Inside this book:

23 illustrated pages, 10 Foil Art pages, and
4 thin foil transfer sheets enclosed in a pocket inside the cover,
plus a sheet of silver stickers for you to decorate your pictures.

Use pencils and the stickers to complete the pictures on the illustrated
pages. You cannot use the thin foil transfer sheets on these pages.

The Foil Art pages are for you to decorate and embellish
with the foil transfer sheets. Please follow the steps below.

✦ Peel away any of the shaded shapes to reveal a sticky surface.

✦ Rub on a foil sheet of your choice, ensuring the foil's dull side
   is face down on the paper, with the bright side **facing up**.

✦ Gently peel away the foil to reveal your foiled picture.

If you need more foil to complete your Foil Art pictures,
thin foil transfer sheets can be
found at most craft stores.

It is Christmas in the heart that puts Christmas in the air.
W. T. Ellis

The Earth has grown old
with its burden of care,
But at Christmas
it always is young;
The heart of the jewel
burns lustrous and fair,
And its soul full of music
breaks forth on the air,
When the song
of angels is sung.

Phillips Brooks

Perhaps the best
Yuletide decoration is
being wreathed in smiles.

Author unknown

'Twas the night before Christmas, when all through the house,
Not a creature was stirring, not even mouse.

Clement Clarke Moore

Christmas is the day
that holds all time together.

Alexander Smith

I heard the bells on Christmas Day
Their old, familiar carols play,
And wild and sweet
The words repeat
Of peace on earth, good-will to men!

Henry Wadsworth Longfellow

Deck the hall
with boughs of holly,
Fa la la la la la la la la la.
'Tis the season to be jolly,
Fa la la la la la la la la la.

Thomas Oliphant

Every gift which is given,
even though it be small,
is in reality great,
if it is given with affection.

Pindar

Nature is full of genius, full of the divinity;
so that not a snowflake escapes its fashioning hand.

Henry David Thoreau

Sing hey!
Sing hey!
For Christmas day;
Twine mistletoe and holly.
For a friendship glows
In winter snows,
And so let's all be jolly!

Author unknown

The holly and the ivy,
now both are full well grown,
Of all the trees
that are in the wood,
the holly bears the crown.

Author unknown

Jingle bells, jingle bells, jingle all the way. Oh what fun it is to ride in a one horse open sleigh.

James Pierpont

Christmas is a season for kindling the fire of hospitality in the hall,
the genial flame of charity in the heart.

Washington Irving

Love came down at Christmas,
Love all lovely, love Divine;
Love was born at Christmas;
Star and angels gave the sign.

Christina Rossetti

At Christmas play and make good cheer,
for Christmas comes but once a year.

Thomas Tusser

May the spirit of Christmas bring you peace,
The gladness of Christmas give you hope,
The warmth of Christmas grant you love.

Author unknown

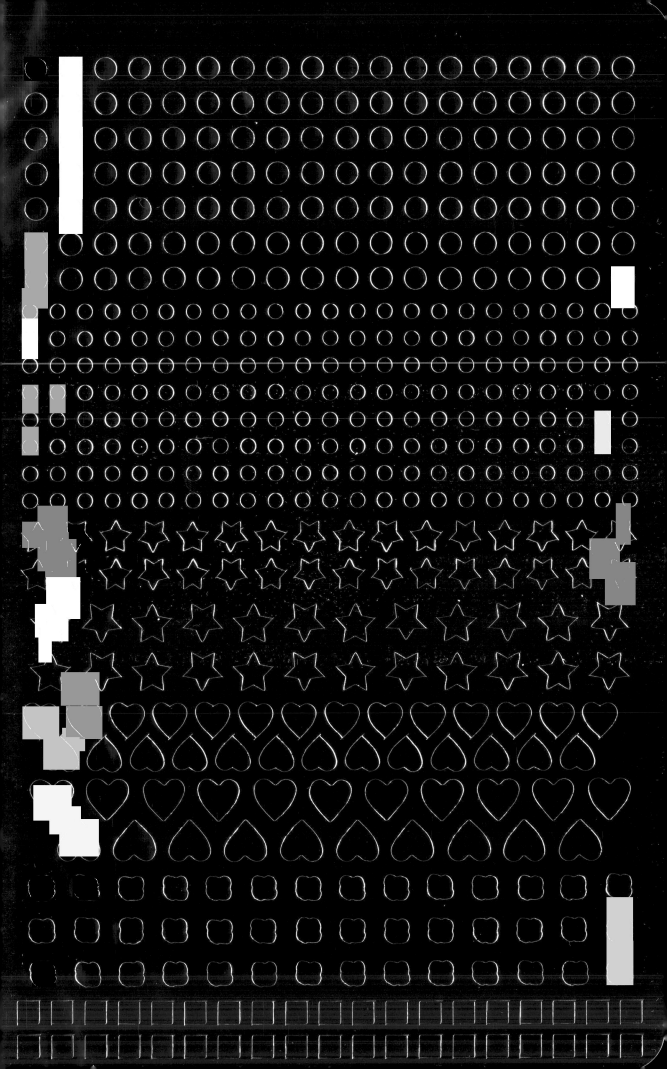